Keeper

Gerald Durrell

Illustrated by Keith West

Michael O'Mara Books Ltd

I am very lucky to have a zoo of my own. My house is in the middle of it, so that all around me live wonderful animals. My dog, who is a boxer, is called Keeper, because he looks after the whole zoo and all the animals are his friends. Every morning he goes out to see them. He makes sure they are well and happy, then comes back to me to tell me how they are.

This morning he woke up in his comfortable basket. He gave several big yawns and stretched his legs. Then he shook himself and came humpety-humpety-hump down the stairs to the kitchen where I was having tea.

'Good morning, Keeper,' I said, 'did you sleep well?'

'Woof,' said Keeper, 'wonderfully,' as he started to eat his breakfast. He likes a big bowl of cornflakes and milk to start with, then a hard-boiled egg. On special days, such as his birthday, he has two hard-boiled eggs.

When he had finished, I said to him, 'I hope you are going out as usual to see that the other animals are all right?'

'Of course,' said Keeper, and off he went.

'Good morning,' shouted all the chittering sparrows, 'Good morning, good morning, where are you going, where are you going?'

'Good morning,' growled Keeper. 'I'm off to see my friends, Dilly and Dally the Penguins.'

'What a beautiful day,' said Keeper to himself. 'I hope everybody else feels as good as I do in the warm sunshine.'

But when he got to the enclosure where Dilly and Dally lived, he found them sitting beside their pool looking very sad.

'Why are you both looking so sad?' asked Keeper. 'It is such a lovely day.'

'Because there is no snow and ice,' said Dilly.

'Where we come from there are icebergs as big as buses and lots of snow and ice,' said Dally.

'But now that spring is here, all the snow and ice have gone,' said Dilly. 'That's why we feel sad.'

'Well, you won't feel sad for long,' said Keeper, 'because I know that today you are going to get fresh water in your pond and it will be really cold.'

The Penguins were delighted at the news.

'Oh, good,' they cried, 'we'll be able to splash about in the icy water and have fun.'

Having cheered up the Penguins, Keeper went off to visit his other friends.

'I'll visit the Tapirs, Claudius and Claudette,' he said to himself. He knew that Claudette had just had a baby, and as he had never seen a baby Tapir, he was most interested. Tapirs live in the forests of South America and are very funny-looking animals. They are a bit like chocolate brown donkeys, but they have long whiffley noses rather like an elephant's trunk. When Claudius saw Keeper he made strange squeaking noises which in Tapir language meant, 'Hello, Keeper, how are you?'

'I'm fine,' said Keeper. 'I've come to see your new baby.'

'He's in our bedroom,' said Claudette. 'I'll call him out for you,' and she gave a loud squeak which in Tapir language meant, 'Come outside, little one, and meet our friend, Keeper.'

When the baby Tapir came out of the house, Keeper was amazed, for though the baby was chocolate brown like his father and mother, it was spotted and streaked with white.

'Goodness gracious!' said Keeper. 'Has somebody splashed paint on your baby?'

'No,' laughed Claudius, 'all baby Tapirs look like that.'

'Why?' asked Keeper.

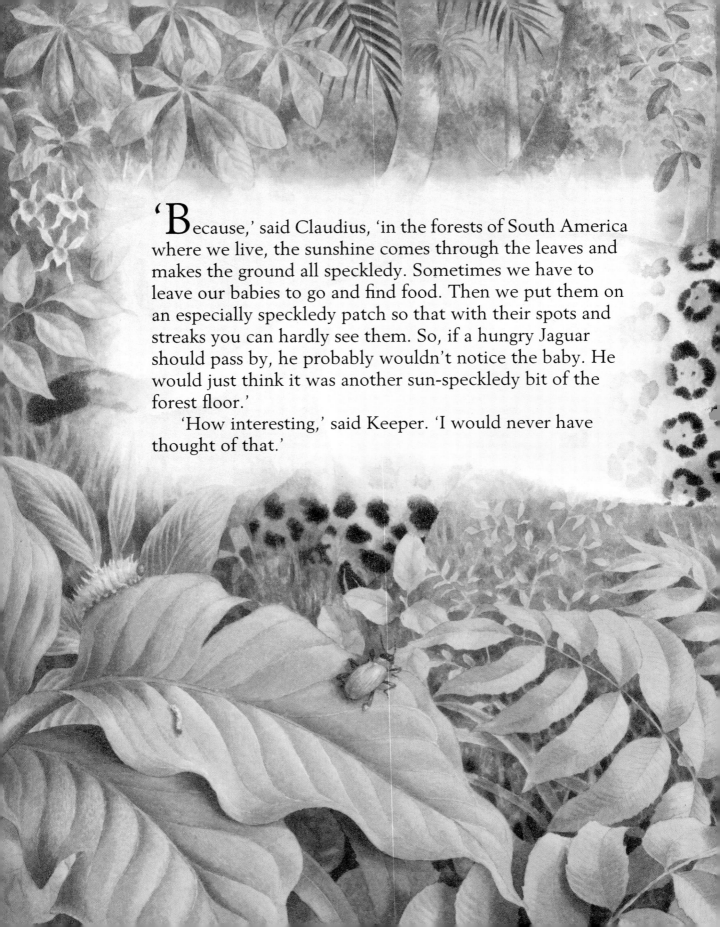

'Because,' said Claudius, 'in the forests of South America where we live, the sunshine comes through the leaves and makes the ground all speckledy. Sometimes we have to leave our babies to go and find food. Then we put them on an especially speckledy patch so that with their spots and streaks you can hardly see them. So, if a hungry Jaguar should pass by, he probably wouldn't notice the baby. He would just think it was another sun-speckledy bit of the forest floor.'

'How interesting,' said Keeper. 'I would never have thought of that.'

Keeper then went to say good morning to the Flamingoes, whose feathers were glowing pink in the sunshine. They were all busy, using their heavy beaks to scoop up mud and pat it into strange-looking piles.

'Hello,' said Keeper. 'What are you doing – making sandcastles?'

'No,' said Daddy Flamingo, 'we're building our nests. You see, they have to be this high to keep them out of the water, and with a deep dent in the top so that they look like a saucepan. This is where we lay our eggs. Then we sit on them and keep them warm until the babies have grown inside the eggs. When we hear them go tickety-tock, tickety-tock, we know it's time for them to hatch. So we watch as they break the shell – tickety-tock, tickety-tock – and climb into the nest.'

'I would like to see that,' thought Keeper. 'Will you tell me when you hear them go tickety-tock?' he asked.

'Of course,' said Daddy Flamingo. 'It's wonderful to see the babies coming out of their shells.'

'It must be like flowers growing – because you have lovely pink feathers and look like a rose bush.'

'No, no,' said Daddy Flamingo. 'When our babies hatch they are grey. It's only later that they get bright pink feathers.'

'Why?' Keeper asked, puzzled.

'If they are grey you don't notice them so much against the mud and water,' said Daddy Flamingo, 'so if there happens to be a hungry Eagle flying overhead he won't see the baby and eat it.'

'Just like the Tapirs,' said Keeper to himself. 'I am learning a lot this morning.'

He went on his way towards the great grassy enclosure where the Gorillas live. Here he saw the big black apes enjoying their breakfast, piles of sweet fruit and crunchy vegetables.

Jambo, the father of the Gorilla family, was huge. His hands were four or five times as big as a man's hand and he weighed as much as three men put together. But although he looked so fierce, he was very gentle and loved his wives and children very much.

'Good morning, Keeper,' said Jambo in his deep, growly voice. 'We are all enjoying the sun. Where we come from in Africa it is always hot. I know we have nice warm bedrooms here, specially heated so that we are comfortable, but there is nothing as good as real sunshine.'

'I agree,' said Keeper. 'A fine day like this makes me feel all bouncy and happy. I'm going to see Pythagoras the Python in the reptile house now, then I'm going down to the lake. I hope you're enjoying your breakfast, Jambo.'

'I am indeed,' growled Jambo. 'This fruit is quite delicious and so is the celery.'

As Keeper trotted off to the reptile house, he thought how surprising it was that by eating just fruit and vegetables, Gorillas could grow up to be so big and strong.

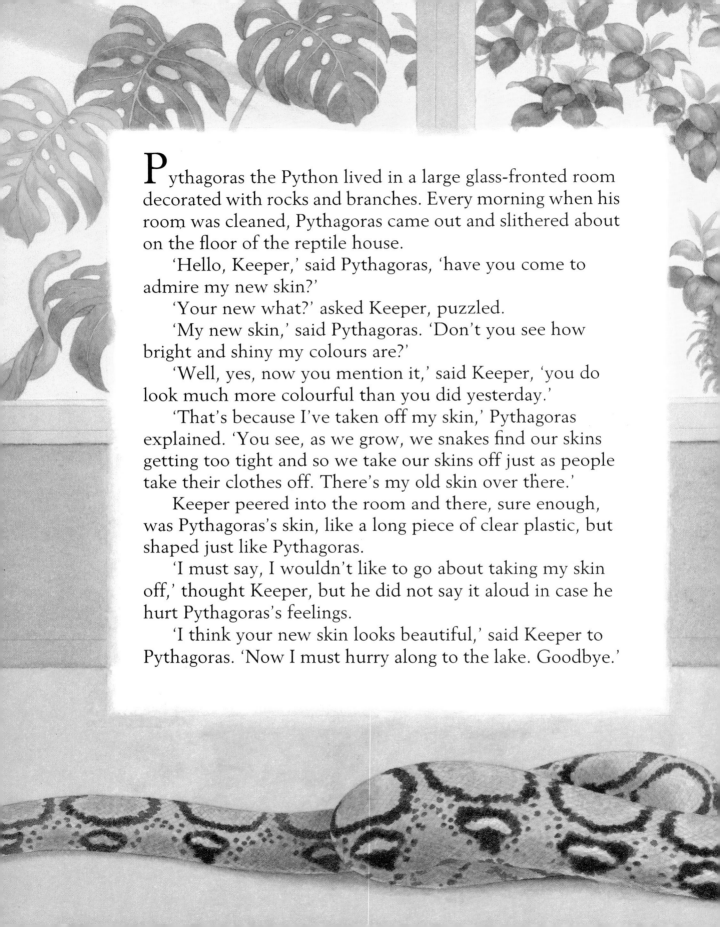

Pythagoras the Python lived in a large glass-fronted room decorated with rocks and branches. Every morning when his room was cleaned, Pythagoras came out and slithered about on the floor of the reptile house.

'Hello, Keeper,' said Pythagoras, 'have you come to admire my new skin?'

'Your new what?' asked Keeper, puzzled.

'My new skin,' said Pythagoras. 'Don't you see how bright and shiny my colours are?'

'Well, yes, now you mention it,' said Keeper, 'you do look much more colourful than you did yesterday.'

'That's because I've taken off my skin,' Pythagoras explained. 'You see, as we grow, we snakes find our skins getting too tight and so we take our skins off just as people take their clothes off. There's my old skin over there.'

Keeper peered into the room and there, sure enough, was Pythagoras's skin, like a long piece of clear plastic, but shaped just like Pythagoras.

'I must say, I wouldn't like to go about taking my skin off,' thought Keeper, but he did not say it aloud in case he hurt Pythagoras's feelings.

'I think your new skin looks beautiful,' said Keeper to Pythagoras. 'Now I must hurry along to the lake. Goodbye.'

As he was going down to the lake, he met Jack, the big black dog from the farm.

'Hello, Jack,' said Keeper. 'Where are you off to?'

'I'm going to the fields to chase rabbits,' said Jack. 'They like being chased in and out of the bramble bushes. I generally do it every morning. The rabbits say that it keeps them warm.'

'Well, one morning I'll join you,' said Keeper, 'but at the moment I must go and see my friends, the Golden Lion Tamarins.'

'What are Tamarins?' asked Jack.

'They're the smallest monkeys in the world,' explained Keeper, 'and they live in South America. The biggest ones are only the size of a kitten and the babies are so tiny that they could fit into a teacup, but they have manes like lions and the most beautiful golden fur you can imagine.'

'Well, I'm off,' said Jack. 'The rabbits are waiting for me.'

Keeper made his way down to the shores of the lake. In the middle of the lake was an island with trees and a little house, where the Tamarins lived.

'Hello,' barked Keeper, and the mother and father Tamarins and their baby all came tumbling out of the house and climbed up into the branches of the trees to twitter, 'Good morning' to Keeper.

'See how much the baby has grown,' said the mother and father Tamarins.

'Look, Keeper,' shouted the baby. 'I don't have to be carried around any longer. I can climb the trees by myself.' And he scampered along a branch to the very end.

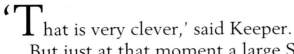

'That is very clever,' said Keeper.

But just at that moment a large Seagull happened to be passing and when it saw the baby Tamarin sitting right on the end of the branch, it thought, 'Now that would make a nice breakfast.'

'Look out! Look out!' shouted the mother and father to the baby. He looked round and saw the enormous Seagull swooping down towards him. He screamed and tried to scramble back to safety, but lost his grip on the branch and fell *splash* into the lake.

'Go away!' shouted Keeper to the Seagull, 'or I'll bite you.'

The Seagull, frightened by Keeper's barks, flew off.

'Oh, Keeper,' shouted the mother and father Tamarins, 'please help our baby! He can't swim.'

The baby was splashing and spluttering in the water. It was clear that he had to be rescued pretty quickly.

'All right, I'm coming,' said Keeper. He dived into the lake and swam across strongly to where the baby Tamarin was struggling. He picked the baby up carefully in his mouth and swam to the island.

'Oh, thank you, thank you,' said the mother and father Tamarins, as Keeper gently put the baby down. 'You've saved our baby's life!'

The baby was none the worse for his wetting, except that he coughed a lot because he had swallowed so much water.

Keeper swam back to the shore and shook himself to get all the drops of water off his fur. Then he came back to the house.

'Well, Keeper,' I said to him, 'what have you been up to?'

'I've learned a lot of very interesting things,' said Keeper, 'about Tapirs and Flamingoes and Snakes and Penguins and Gorillas.'

'You've been in the water,' I said.

Keeper shook himself, and told me about the baby Tamarin and the rescue.

'It was nothing,' he said.

'It was a very brave thing to do,' I said. 'You look after the animals very well.'

'That's my job,' said my dog. 'That's why I'm called Keeper.'